MW00909587

Things That Go Bark In The Park

**More Devilish Fun with C.D. Bitesky, Howie Wolfner,
Elisa and Frankie Stein, and Danny Keegan**
From Avon Camelot

FIFTH GRADE MONSTER SERIES
M Is For Monster
Born To Howl
The Pet Of Frankenstein
There's A Batwing In My Lunchbox
Z Is For Zombie
Monster Mashers
Yuckers!

Coming Soon
The Monster In Creeps Head Bay

Things That Go Bark In The Park

Mel Gilden

Illustrated by John Pierard

A GLC BOOK

AN AVON CAMELOT BOOK

THINGS THAT GO BARK IN THE PARK is an original publication of Avon Books. This work has never before appeared in book form.

AVON BOOKS
A division of
The Hearst Corporation
105 Madison Avenue
New York, New York 10016

Text and illustrations copyright © 1989 by General Licensing Company, Inc.
Published by arrangement with General Licensing Company, Inc.
Developed by Byron Preiss and Dan Weiss
Library of Congress Catalog Card Number: 89-91299
ISBN: 0-380-75786-9
RL: 4.9

First Avon Camelot Printing: October 1989

CAMELOT TRADEMARK REG. U.S. PAT. OFF. AND IN OTHER COUNTRIES, MARCA REGISTRADA. HECHO EN U.S.A.

Printed in the U.S.A.

OPM   10   9   8   7   6   5   4   3   2

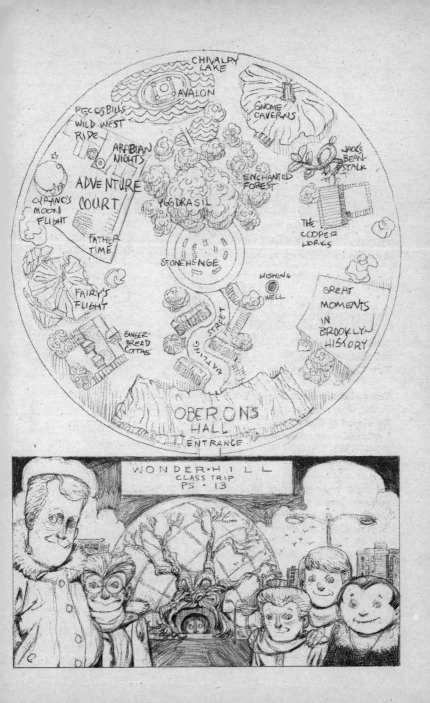

Chapter One

Gather Round, Spirits, Gather Round

Danny Keegan was sitting on the floor of Howie Wolfner's room with the Sunday comics before him, but he wasn't reading them or even looking at the pictures. Danny was wondering how he got himself into these things.

Innocently enough, Danny had come over to read the comics with Howie. And now, just because it would be "jolly good fun," Howie had called the rest of Danny's monster friends, inviting them to participate in something that really shouldn't bother Danny because it probably wouldn't work anyway.

Howie walked into the room carrying a big silver pitcher and two big glasses, each of which had a noble dog figure on the side. Gamboling at his heels was a mechanical dog made entirely of brass. The dog trotted across the newspapers and licked Danny once with his dry, papery tongue. "Down, Bruno," Danny said. Bruno lay down next to Danny and thumped his tail against the floor.

1

"Orange juice?" Howie said, holding the sweating pitcher aloft.

"Sure, thanks," Danny said. In a single smooth motion, Howie sank to the floor and poured two glasses of juice. Bruno sniffed them both, decided that orange juice wasn't for him, and lay down again.

Danny took a sip and said, "You really think this'll work?"

"We must know the truth," Howie said in his English accent. He was not any bigger than the average fifth grader at P.S. 13, but he was much stronger, and he could do things on a skateboard that Danny had not seen anybody else do outside a circus. He had a lot of reddish brown hair that came to a point between his thick eyebrows. His nose always had a black smudge on it. The smudge was not dirt.

"I guess," said Danny, not convinced.

Bruno watched with interest while they passed around sections of the paper. Soon Howie's room was a city of newspaper tents and high rises. Howie had given Bruno the classified ads to tussle with. Shreds of newspaper flew everywhere as Bruno showed the classifieds who was boss. From the living room came the sound of the football game Mr. Wolfner was watching on TV. Sometimes Mr. Wolfner cried, "Jolly good!" and sometimes he cried even louder, "Bloomin' idjit!" Danny imagined his father making similar comments at the Keegan house.

Danny read through the comics, skipping the soap opera ones because they were so-o-o-o boring, then traded with Howie for the TV listings.

They both looked up when the doorbell rang and Bruno trotted off to see who was at the door. A moment later he returned, herding Danny's other monster friends. The Stein kids leaned against either side of the doorway, and C.D. Bitesky looked between them into the room.

C.D. Bitesky was short, but very charming. When he smiled, two tiny fangs showed. As usual, he was wearing a tuxedo, complete with a cape lined with red satin. His hair was glassy and almost looked as if it were painted on. In his rolling Transylvanian way he said, "Good morning," and bowed.

"Hi, guys," Danny said.

"It is quite nasty outside," C.D. said.

"Snow will fall soon," Frankie said.

When he was standing, Frankie Stein was almost as tall as some of the teachers at P.S. 13. His hair was more like black grass, and it refused to be combed. He always had a plastic pen holder in his shirt pocket and a selection of pens of different colors. Like his sister, he had a knob on either side of his neck. Ms. Cosgrove, their teacher, thought the knobs had something to do with a neck injury. They did not.

Elisa Stein was a little shorter than Frankie, but much neater. A gray streak, like a lightning bolt, stood out on her hair just above her ears.

Frankie knelt and patted Bruno. It sounded as if he were patting a bell. "Bruno looks as if he is working fine."

"Tip-top," Howie said.

Frankie frowned and pulled a small screwdriver from his pocket. "Perhaps a minor adjustment," he said.

Howie said, "I appreciate your giving Bruno to me, Frankie, and certainly no one else could have put him together. But may I suggest a course of action? If it isn't broken, don't fix it."

Frankie sighed and put away his screwdriver.

Elisa said, "On the telephone, you mentioned a seance."

"Quite right," Howie said. "Take a look at this." He crawled through the newspaper city, looking for something. "Ah," he said, holding the local news section up to Elisa.

Frankie looked over her shoulder as she read aloud, " 'Amusement Park Opening Day Set.' "

"What means this?" C.D. said.

"Amusement park?" said Danny. "You know— like Disneyland."

"Ah, yes." C.D. nodded and pulled a thermos from a pocket inside his cape, and began to suck Fluid of Life from it through a straw. "We have such places in the old country."

"Draculand," Howie said and laughed.

C.D. shook his head and said, "Sometimes, with the tourists, it seems that you are correct."

"Listen to this," Elisa said. " 'After years of broken promises, Wonder Hill, an amusement park planned and financed by millionaire Roland Hill, is due to open next month.' "

"Hah," said Danny, sneering. "I've heard that before."

"I am only reading what it says," said Elisa. " 'Despite the constant stream of workers who walked off the job claiming that the place was haunted, Hill insists, "These things are open to interpretation." ' The story goes on."

4

"Allow me to see," C.D. said, pulling the paper down to his level.

Danny had seen the picture. Wonder Hill was entirely protected by a big dome. From the outside, it looked like a golf ball half buried in the ground, but it was a golf ball almost ten stories high. In one corner of the Wonder Hill picture, a photo of Roland Hill was inset. Hill had pudgy cheeks, and his sandy hair was combed over to one side. The narrow mustache didn't really make him look any older; he still looked like a high school kid with a mustache.

C.D. let go of the paper and said, "What did you have in your brain, Howie?"

Howie looked from side to side, as if he expected somebody to be listening down chimneys and through keyholes. He leaned toward Frankie and Elisa and C.D. and said, "I propose we hold a seance, find out if Wonder Hill is really haunted, and if it is, banish the ghost."

"In other words," Danny said, "he wants to get us haunted too."

"No, no, Danny. That isn't it at all. A seance is a ceremony during which we can communicate with ghosts and spirits. We will talk to whomever is haunting Wonder Hill, and politely ask him or her to go away. It's all very diplomatic and civilized."

"However," said Frankie, "it is not very scientific."

"Balderdash, old man. It could not be more scientific."

C.D. said, "My family is not concerned much with ghosts. However, I will help if I can."

5

"Jolly good. All we need now is a medium—someone to lead the seance."

In the other room, the crowd on the TV roared, and Mr. Wolfner shouted, "Good show!"

Danny would have volunteered, but he had no idea how to be a medium. Evidently, the others felt the same way because they shuffled their feet and looked expectantly at Howie. For once, Howie was not comfortable being the center of attention. Then Elisa said, "I will do it."

"You will?" Howie seemed surprised.

"She has had experience," Frankie said.

Dreamily, looking through the room before her, Elisa said, "There was that time in Germany . . ." Then she cut herself off with a shake of her head and said, "Where will we do it?"

Howie opened his arms wide and said, "I leave it to you."

Elisa nodded and said, "What about the observatory?"

"Capital."

Elisa folded the newspaper under her arm and led them out of the room. Bruno followed them along a short hallway and then up a spiral staircase that rose at the end of it. The staircase took them up to a circular room no bigger than Howie's bedroom but much colder. A telescope pointed skyward, but the slit in the ceiling that would allow it a view of the sky was presently closed.

A single narrow cylinder of light shone on a round table in the center of the room. At it sat a pretty woman who had long hair falling to her shoulders like waves of silver. On her lavender sweatshirt was the legend FULL MOON MAMA. She

6

was doing math with the help of a pocket calculator. The light threw strange shadows of the woman and of the telescope onto the high domed ceiling.

"Ah, Mrs. Wolfner," C.D. said. He stepped forward, took her hand and kissed it. Mrs. Wolfner barely got the pencil out of her hand before he poked himself in the eye. "Hello, C.D., kids. Hello, Bruno." The dog set his forepaws on her legs and panted at her.

"Are you working up here, Mum?" Howie said.

"Just finished. Is your father still watching football?"

"If one is to believe the prehistoric sounds coming from the living room."

"I find those sounds difficult to believe even when I hear them myself. I'll see if I can't spirit him away to the mall. Some wonderful lamps are on sale."

"Could you take Bruno downstairs with you? We have important things to do."

"Don't break anything."

"We won't touch any of the equipment."

"Very well. Come along, Bruno. I have some nice electrons for you." Bruno leaped to the stairs, wagging his tail. Mrs. Wolfner gathered her papers and her calculator together and descended, her running shoes going *thunk thunk* on the spiral stairs, Bruno leading the way.

"Now," said Elisa mysteriously, "everyone take a seat at the table." The kids did as they were told, and Elisa set the newspaper in the middle, with the pictures of Wonder Hill and Roland Hill under the bright light.

"I have the creeps," C.D. said.

7

"Fear not," said Frankie. "This is a place of science."

Danny knew Frankie was right. He had spent many interesting evenings in this room with Howie and his parents and the others, looking at the moon and the stars and other planets. But C.D. was right. That didn't prevent it from being creepy. It was too dark, too cold, too full of half-seen spidery scientific instruments.

"We must hold hands," Elisa said.

Danny took Elisa's hand on one side and C.D.'s hand on the other. Their hands were cold. His were probably cold too. It meant nothing.

Elisa said, "Now we must concentrate on the photograph of Wonder Hill. Nothing else must exist for us."

Danny looked at the photo. He was seeing it from the side and Wonder Hill looked more like a half-buried golf ball than ever. He tried not to think of golf balls but of great domed amusement parks, of all the great rides inside, something or somebody who was haunting the place. He had to blink to keep the picture in focus. On either side, hands were tight in his.

The observatory was very quiet but for the gentle ticking of the clockwork that aimed the telescope. Danny thought he could hear the breathing of the others so well that he could sort them out, tell which whispering sound belonged to whom.

Something tickled his hands and went through his entire body. It was such a vague feeling that at first he wasn't even sure he'd felt anything. But it got stronger. It felt like electricity running up his arms and across his shoulders. It seemed to rush both ways at once, like expressway traffic in the middle of the night. He was afraid to look up from the photo of Wonder Hill for fear he would somehow ruin whatever was happening.

Elisa spoke. Her voice was low and kind of a moan. It was deeper than usual, as if she had a sore throat. It barely sounded like Elisa at all. She said, "Gather round, spirits. Gather round. We search for one who haunts this place, unable to rest."

The electricity through Danny's body was almost unbearable. It didn't hurt, but it created an enormous expectant tension—like the tension you feel when you sit down in a dentist's chair or when it's your turn to talk during the school play, or when you're in a big store and you realize suddenly that you've wandered away from your parents. It was like that but stronger. Anything could happen next.

Wind rushed through the observatory and lifted the corners of the newspaper. The wind blew harder and moved the newspaper, then harder still; the paper slid across the table and fell to the floor with a crash, as if it were made of glass. Danny continued to stare at the empty spot where the paper had been.

A voice spoke. It echoed as if it came from a long distance and wavered as if the person speaking were making a great effort to do it. "Curse you," the voice said. Danny looked up. He could not help himself. He looked up and saw a long tunnel of spiraling smoke. At the end of it was a man dressed like somebody during the Revolutionary War. The man spun closer, and

9

then retreated, then came closer again. He looked angry.

"Curse you, Overton Hill! Curse you."

"Who is Overton Hill?" Elisa said.

"Curse you," the man said.

"We offer help," Elisa said. "But we must know who Overton Hill is."

"Curse you, Overton Hill," the man said, then spun off into the darkness. The smoke spun after him like water down a drain.

"Wait," Elisa shouted, but whether she commanded the kids or the spirit man, Danny didn't know. He held on tight. He felt like time had stopped, and he might stay frozen like this forever.

"Come back," Elisa said. "We must know who Overton Hill is or we cannot help you."

Nothing happened. The electricity in Danny's body was gone. He became aware that Elisa and C.D. were gripping his hands so tightly they hurt. As if at a signal, everybody let go at once. Elisa slumped back in her chair, her eyes closed. Frankie picked up the paper from the floor. Something had burned a hole right in the center of the Wonder Hill dome.

The kids looked at each other.

His voice shaking, Howie said, "Instead of answers, we seem to have a few more questions."

Chapter Two

Stevie's Show-and-Tell

The kids just sat there for a while. The room was creepier than ever. It seemed to be a big living thing that had eaten them. The big shadows that crowded the curved walls now loomed like mysterious tunnels to the dark unknown.

Frankie and Danny each took one of Elisa's hands and rubbed her wrists, hoping that would revive her. A few minutes later, her eyelids fluttered. Elisa sat up and said, "Thank you."

"Are you all right?" Howie said.

"I would appreciate a glass of water."

"Water. Right."

But nobody moved. Danny knew what the problem was. Moving would take you away from the safety of the table, of the chairs, of good friends. It might bring back that strange guy. At last C.D. said, "What does it mean?"

Elisa swallowed and said, "I don't know. I don't even know if that's the spirit haunting Wonder Hill, or . . . or what." Her voice was thick, as if she'd just awakened.

Howie said, "That outfit was from the late eighteenth century, about the time of the American Revolutionary War. Don't you think, Danny?"

"Could have been," Danny said. "I'm no expert."

"I'm for the encyclopedia," Howie said, and leaped up. Before anybody could say anything, he was halfway down the stairs. Danny rose with everybody else and followed. Howie wasn't there when they entered the library.

"Howie?" C.D. said, a little worried.

"Right here," said Howie. He rushed into the room with a big glass of water. Bruno followed him in and made a snuffling sound as he settled in a corner, watching everything. Gratefully, Elisa took the glass and sipped the water as Howie took down volume one of the encyclopedia. He looked everywhere he could think of, but could find no reference to Overton Hill.

"Maybe he did not exist," C.D. said.

"Or maybe he was just some guy who never made it into the history books," Danny said.

Frankie said, "Through my computer modem I have access to much information."

Elisa nodded and said, "Any who wish to come and observe the search are welcome."

"Perhaps some other time," C.D. said, bowing. "I, for one, wish to be home before dark."

"You got that right," Danny said.

He, C.D., and the Stein kids went home after that. And though the sun was shining on familiar territory, Danny found that everything on the bus ride home reminded him of ghosts and spirits and seances. He wondered who Overton Hill was and why anybody would want to curse him.

Snow was beginning to fall as Danny walked to school the next day with his sister, Barbara. Their cheeks were rubbed red by the cold wind, and Danny felt small as he hunched into his warm clothes.

Danny hadn't told anybody about the adventure in Howie's observatory the day before, and he'd kept to himself a lot. If he told them about the seance, his parents would just ask a lot of questions and congratulate him on the powers of his imagination. As it was, his mom had taken his temperature.

Now Barbara said, "What's the story, Danny?"

But Danny didn't tell her. He didn't want *her* asking him any questions either. Not yet. Not till he had more answers. Not till some of the fear had worn off.

The school yard was empty. Everybody was huddled against the walls of P.S. 13, trying to stay out of the wind. Barbara ran off to her fourth grade class, and Danny joined the other members of Ms. Cosgrove's fifth grade class.

Jason Nickles walked up to him and said, "You want a ticket to Wonder Hill?"

Danny was suspicious, but he said, "Yeah, sure."

Jason quickly ran his finger up a deck of cards, flicking them at Danny right under his nose. A couple of the other kids laughed, and Jason got away before Danny could grab him. Jason went to stand with Stevie Brickwald, who was whispering something to Angela Marconi.

"Whatever Stevie is telling Angela will be all over the school soon."

Still fuming over Jason's trick, Danny turned and saw C.D. standing next to him. C.D. was wrapped in a long black cape, and he was wearing a round Russian fur hat, with flaps down over the ears.

"Yeah," said Danny. "Here she comes now."

As soon as she was in calling distance, she said, "I know a secret, but I'm not supposed to tell."

"That's OK, Angela. C.D. and I understand."

"I wouldn't tell you even if you asked," Angela said.

C.D. bowed.

Angela whispered, "If you promise not to tell, I'll tell."

"Better not, Angela. It's a secret."

Angela said, "I know something about Stevie Brickwald you don't know," and giggled as she ran to where Laurie Perry was talking to Ruth Ashly.

"She did not tell us," C.D. said with surprise.

Danny said, "Stevie probably told her he's from Mars."

"Yes," said C.D. seriously. "And I would believe it too. He is very like a Martian."

Howie and the Stein kids showed up. Frankie said that he'd checked various data bases but had not been able to find any reference to Overton Hill. "He is obscure," Frankie said.

"Obscure or not," said Howie, "he's made someone very angry."

The playground took on a dingy forbidding cast, and when the bell rang, Danny and the other monster kids jumped. They were all glad to go inside. Once in Ms. Cosgrove's classroom, kids peeled off layer after layer of clothing, and soon the cloakroom looked like the base camp for a trek across the Arctic ice.

When Stevie Brickwald removed his coat, he attracted a crowd.

"I don't want to know," Danny said, as he headed for his seat.

"Assuredly not," Howie said.

"Everybody please take his or her seat," Ms. Cosgrove called.

When the crowd around Stevie broke up, Danny could see that he was wearing a yellow sweatshirt. Painted on the front was a picture of a half-buried golf ball and the words "Wonder Hill" written in fancy fantasy script.

"Well," said Howie. "That is rum news."

"Yeah," said Danny. "If Stevie Brickwald is the first kid in school to have a Wonder Hill shirt, we'll never hear the end of it."

For show-and-tell, three kids had brought in the article from the Sunday paper about Wonder Hill, and Ms. Cosgrove let them take turns talking about it. When they were done, Stevie Brickwald kind of casually raised his hand, and Ms. Cosgrove called on him.

Stevie swaggered to the front of the room and said, "I just want all of you to know that Roland Hill, the millionaire and the brains behind Wonder Hill, is my uncle Roland."

Silence fell.

Danny whispered to Howie, "That must be Angela's secret." Howie nodded.

Ms. Cosgrove said, "Is that true, Stevie?"

"Of course it's true. What do you think I am, anyway?"

Jason Nickles called out, "Give us a break, Stevie."

A lot of kids grumbled, "Yeah, Stevie. Give us a break."

"It's true, and I can prove it." Stevie folded his arms across his chest, realized he was hiding the Wonder Hill picture, and unfolded his arms.

"How will you prove it, Stevie?" Ms. Cosgrove asked.

Stevie waited until he had everybody's attention. He said, "I will bring Uncle Roland in for show-and-tell."

Ms. Cosgrove sighed. "That's fine, Stevie. We'll all look forward to that, won't we class?"

There was a chorus of very nasty yeahs. Stevie did not appear to be worried.

At recess, Marla Willaby siddled up to Stevie and tugged the sleeve of his shirt. She said, "Gee, Stevie, maybe you and I could go to Wonder Hill sometime, hmmm?" She smiled into his face and batted her eyelashes. Evidently, she was taking no chances that Stevie's claim might not be true. A lot of other kids were taking no chances either.

Danny and his friends met under their tree and watched most of Ms. Cosgrove's class approach Stevie, trying to be his friend.

"It's disgusting. He's acting like a king or something," Danny said.

"Indeed," Howie said. "One might say he is holding court."

Elisa said, "I, for one, do not believe him."

17

"You are very wise," C.D. said, "for a girl who has not yet lived even one lifetime."

Howie said, "If Stevie brings anybody for show-and-tell, it will be some impostor."

"I don't know," Danny said. "Stevie'd have to be pretty dumb to do that after Roland Hill's picture was in the paper yesterday."

Elisa said, "Perhaps Stevie thinks that *we* are pretty dumb."

"Perhaps," C.D. said and sipped his Fluid of Life.

The snow continued to fall for the next few days, but it fell lazily, as if it knew it had all winter to empty the clouds. Danny's breath frosted the air as he ran up the stairs of P.S. 13 hoping he wasn't late. He managed to get his heavy clothes off and sit down just as Ms. Cosgrove called for volunteers for show-and-tell. Agnes Tone made a dime disappear, and Arthur Finster showed off a leaf that looked like the profile of Mickey Mouse.

Then Ms. Cosgrove called on Stevie. He strolled to the front of the room with his hands in his pockets. Danny did not think he was going to show off magic tricks or fancy leaves. He was smirking too self-confidently for that. When he got to the front he just stood there.

"Go on, Stevie," Ms. Cosgrove said.

Without saying anything, Stevie walked to the door, opened it, and went out. A moment later, he returned with a man wearing a gray suit. Danny blinked. He couldn't believe his eyes.

Stevie said, "Here he is, guys. My uncle Roland Hill."

The class erupted into noisy chatter. Danny was convinced there was a trick here somewhere, and he was not alone. Still, the guy did look like the picture of Roland Hill that had been in the paper. If it was a trick, it was a good one—better than making a dime disappear.

"Please, class," Ms. Cosgrove called out. Then, in a more polite voice, she said, "Good morning, Mr. Hill. How nice of you to visit us."

"It's my pleasure, I'm sure."

"May we ask you questions?"

"Of course."

While this had been going on, Stevie had been standing to one side smiling hard enough to break his face. He shook his fist in the air in triumph.

Jason Nickles said, "Are you really Roland Hill?"

"I am. Want to see my driver's license?" He laughed pleasantly.

"The millionaire who built Wonder Hill?" Angela Marconi said in a breathless voice.

Still smiling, Hill raised one hand and said, "That's me. I confess."

Danny looked over at Marla Willaby, but she was leaning on the palm of one hand, a dreamy look in her eyes, worshipping Mr. Hill from afar.

Howie raised his hand, and Mrs. Cosgrove called on him. Howie said, "Are you acquainted with someone named Overton Hill?"

"Why, yes. As a matter of fact, I am."

Surprised glances bounced among Danny and the monster kids.

Mr. Hill went on, "He is an ancestor of mine—Stevie's and mine. As a matter of fact, he used to own most of the land where Wonder Hill now stands." Mr. Hill chuckled. "I understand from my historians that he was a hardheaded no-nonsense kind of businessman. I'm surprised you've heard of him."

"Oh," said Howie, "I do a lot of reading." Howie glanced at Danny. Danny shrugged.

"Was there anything else, Howie?" Ms. Cosgrove said.

"Not at this time. No."

Ms. Cosgrove said, "You have a question, Elisa?"

"Yes, Ms. Cosgrove. I would like to know if there is truth in any of the rumors we hear."

The smile melted off Mr. Hill's face like spring snow. "Rumors?" he said.

"Yes sir. We hear much of hauntings."

Mr. Hill shrugged and said, "Just coincidence and unfounded rumors. I assure you that nothing is going on at Wonder Hill that cannot be explained." He snapped his fingers and went on, "As a matter of fact, I'll prove it to you." He turned to Stevie and said, "Stevie, I'd like to invite you and your class to visit Wonder Hill on the day before the park opens to the public. Convince yourselves that there is nothing there in the least supernatural. Nothing we haven't built in on purpose, anyway." His good spirits seemed to have returned.

The members of the class turned as one to Ms. Cosgrove. Howie said, "I'm sure it would be educational."

"What do you think, Stevie?" Ms. Cosgrove said.

"Sure," said Stevie. "If my uncle Roland built

it, you can bet it'll be more educational than anything. And fun too."

Trying to suppress a smile, Ms. Cosgrove said, "Well. Educational and fun too. We can't pass up an opportunity like that. All right, Mr. Hill. We'd be delighted."

The class cheered.

Chapter Three

The Hounds of Heck

At recess, Danny said, "I expected Mr. Hill to be the same kind of creep as Stevie."

C.D. pulled his Fluid of Life from his cape and sucked on it for a moment before he said, "Perhaps Stevie is the black cow of the family."

"Isn't a black cow like a root beer float?" Howie said.

"Yeah," Danny said. "I think C.D. means black sheep."

"Ah, yes," C.D. said. "I knew it was a black farm animal." He bowed to Danny. Danny found it impossible not to bow back.

Howie pounded his fist into his palm and said, "One of us should have asked Mr. Hill about the curse."

C.D. smiled, showing his fangs, and said, "We are all too cautious to ask before the entire class."

"We have no proof, after all," said Frankie.

"No proof to others, perhaps," Elisa said. "But we know now that we did not imagine the appearance of the strange man. It is unlikely our imaginations, even if working as one, would make up a name that in reality is so closely connected to Wonder Hill."

Danny said, "Somehow, proof that we had a run-in with a real ghost doesn't make me feel any better."

"Ah, Danny," Howie said. "A ghost is just one more kind of monster. By now, you should be an expert dealing with monsters."

Danny nodded. "Still," he said, " 'there are the good and the bad,' as the pirates say."

"We are going to Wonder Hill," Howie said. "That is good enough for me."

As much as he wanted to go to Wonder Hill, Danny dreaded the day he took his trip permission slip home. As it turned out, his worst fears were not quite realized at the dinner table.

His sister, Barbara, said, "Why can't I go?"

"Because you're not in my class, doofus."

"Mom, Danny called me a doofus."

"Danny, don't call your sister a doofus."

"But, Mom! She can't go. She's not in Ms. Cosgrove's class."

Mrs. Keegan looked across the pot roast and string beans and potatoes at her husband and said, "You're mighty quiet."

Mr. Keegan gently put down his fork and said, "Well, Barbara, I guess Danny's right."

"I'm not a doofus."

Mr. Keegan went on calmly. "You're not a doofus, Barb, but you're not in Ms. Cosgrove's class either. Only kids in Ms. Cosgrove's class are going to Wonder Hill."

"It's not fair. And I don't like pot roast anyway."

Danny failed to see what one thing had to do with the other.

Mrs. Keegan said, "You know, Barbara, I'll bet it'll take a couple of weeks for them to get Wonder Hill perfect."

"What do you mean?" she said suspiciously.

"It's like with a new car," Mrs. Keegan said. "You have to drive it for a while and listen to all the creaks and grinds and decide which of them needs fixing."

"You mean Danny'll be going to a broken park?"

"Kind of," Mrs. Keegan said.

"How long will it take them to fix it?" Barbara said.

"I don't know," Mrs. Keegan said.

"A few weeks. A month," Mr. Keegan said.

"Can we go to Wonder Hill then?"

"I guess," Mr. Keegan said.

"And Danny can't go because he already went once."

"But it'll be broken when I go," Danny said.

"Oh, yeah."

The argument was pretty much over at that point and Danny sighed with relief. Danny was not always comfortable with his parents' concepts of justice. For a minute there, he'd worried that his parents wouldn't let him go unless Barbara went too.

Days went by. Snow lay ever deeper on the ground. Danny was afraid that the world would end—or worse—before he had a chance to see Wonder Hill. Then one morning he and his class took the long bus ride to the edge of Brooklyn. Laughter on the bus was frequent, and there was much telling of jokes.

"There it is," Frankie said at last, pointing out the window. Looming above the apartment buildings was the giant dome. Everybody watched it as the bus wound through the streets and then pulled up to the front gates.

"All right, everybody," Ms. Cosgrove said, but her class needed no encouragement. Danny and the others climbed to the ground and stood there, not quite believing they'd arrived at last.

The main gate of Wonder Hill looked like an enormous wooden door embedded in a gigantic tree whose branches wound halfway up the side of the dome. It opened slowly from the center, pushing against pillows of snow. Finally Mr. Roland Hill walked out looking very small indeed. "Hurry inside," he said. "Hurry."

When they'd all gotten inside the dome and the doors closed, Mr. Hill said, "I didn't realize it was so cold out there." He was rubbing his hands together, and Danny noticed that the heavy clothes which had seemed just right outside, now made him feel scratchy, overheated, and nervous.

They were standing inside an enormous hall with a low dirt ceiling from which roots dangled between the beams. Along the walls were electric torches that flickered as if they were real fire. Between the torches were round shields and crossed swords and hunting horns hanging from pegs. Diamonds and jewels and chunks of gold that glowed with their own light were piled up in corners. Not far away, Danny could hear a crowd dancing to the joyful sound of bagpipes and flutes and drums.

Mr. Hill took the class through a cloakroom, where there was enough room to hang thousands of coats and hats. Now that he no longer had his heavy clothes on, Danny could feel the air of Wonder Hill against his skin. It had the quality of a soft spring day.

On the other side of the cloakroom they walked along a stone passageway from which they could look down through a picture window at elves dancing and turning somersaults and hanging from torches and drinking and eating as the ancient pagan music continued. To one side, an elf wearing a crown of glittering twigs sat on a throne which had the heads of monsters for arms. He moved his gold cup in time with the music. "Oberon, king of the elves," Ms. Cosgrove said, reading a sign at the front of the window.

"Eat your heart out, Mr. Price," Howie whispered to Danny. Danny nodded. Mr. Price ran Brooklyn's wax museum. His exibits looked chintzy and cheap compared to Oberon's throne room.

A little farther on, another elf stood over the arch of the tunnel and between swallows from his cup, he said, "Welcome to Wonder Hill. Have a good time. You'll be here a while." The elf laughed.

"What does he mean by that?" Howie said.

Ms. Cosgrove said, "It's said that while a person spent one night having a good time inside the mountain home of fairies and elves, a hundred years passed outside."

"Oohh," they all said together.

It was funny, Danny thought. He didn't believe he'd be stuck inside Wonder Hill for a hundred years, but it was fun to think he might be. Being scared could be fun, if you knew that there was really nothing to be scared of. Maybe that was why people went to places like Wonder Hill and to horror movies.

There was one more bend in the tunnel, and then they stood at the foot of a crooked street. A sign shaped like a finger told them this was Watling Street. The street was lined with thatched huts, and at its far end was a tree that looked as if its branches scratched the top of the dome.

In the expectant silence, Danny could hear a soft moaning and squeaking, as if a giant were turning over in a huge bed somewhere in the park.

Mr. Hill said, "This is Watling Street, the main street of Wonder Hill. The real Watling Street was an ancient Roman road that crossed England from one side to the other. Each hut you see is actually a store or a restaurant. They're not open at the moment, but the rides are all ready to run on automatic. At the far end of Watling Street you can see Yggdrasil, a monstrous tree that, according to Norse legend, is said to hold the universe together with its roots. In front of it is a full-scale model of Stonehenge, the center of the park, and a mystical mysterious place."

Ruth Ashly asked, "What's that creaking noise?"

"Not to worry," Mr. Hill said. "The dome is under some stress because of the wind blowing outside and because of the snow piled on top. But the engineers who built this place took all that into account. They assure me Wonder Hill could withstand an ice age."

"You promised this would be an educational experience as well as a fun one," Ms. Cosgrove said. She sounded serious, but she could not help smiling.

"Right," said Mr. Hill. "First stop, Great Moments in Brooklyn History."

"Great," said Ms. Cosgrove, ignoring the groans of her class. Mr. Hill led them in the direction of Yggdrasil.

As they walked up Watling Street, Danny saw a woodcutter's hut, Titania's Jewelry Shoppe, and Chaucer's Inn. To one side was a mountain with enormous diamonds stuck into it like chocolate chips in a cookie. "Fairy's Flight, anybody?" Danny said, reading the sign on a nearby ride.

"Roller coasters are for wimps," Stevie said contemptuously. "All you do is sit there. I like the bumper barrels in the Cooper Works." It figured that Stevie would have already tried all the rides himself.

"I am curious to see Father Time's time travel ride," said Elisa.

"I'm for Pecos Bill's Wild West Stagecoach ride," cried Howie.

As they walked, they were spreading out, each kid eager to explore the park. "Stay together, class," Ms. Cosgrove said.

Then, far off, Danny heard dogs howling and barking. Everybody stopped and listened. There it came again. Howie sniffed the air.

"What's that?" Ms.Cosgrove said.

Mr. Hill laughed in an unconvincing way and said, "Special effects, that's all. Just special effects."

"I don't think so," Howie grumbled. Danny

looked at him, and saw Frankie and Elisa and C.D. looking at him too.

"Come on, kids," said Ms. Cosgrove. "Great Moments in Brooklyn History awaits us."

But the howling and barking was getting closer and nobody moved. All Danny's senses were quivering, and he was ready to fight or run, whichever seemed to be a better idea. Suddenly a pack of dogs, each the size of a small horse and the color of hot, mottled autumn leaves, bounded around the corner of Oberon's Magic Shoppe and headed for the group.

Everybody began to run back to the arch where the class had come in, but the loping dogs were too quick. They circled the group. The kids, now shrieking and crying with fear, backed together into a tight bunch in the center of Watling Street with Ms. Cosgrove and Mr. Hill on the outside trying to protect them.

One of the dogs leaped at Howie, but shied away. Another leaped at Danny, but instead of ripping him to shreds with its big sharp teeth, the dog glared at him with its fiery eyes and breathed on him with its warm rancid doggy breath. It roughly sniffed him all over, tickling Danny with its big bulb of a cold nose, which felt like a wet potato. Then the dog ran off and sniffed somebody else.

"Hounds of Heck!" Howie shouted.

"What?" said Danny. "I just made that up so my dog, Harryhauser, would have a costume last Halloween."

"Sorry, old man," Howie said. "You may have invented them independently, but they really exist, and there they are."

"Where do they come from?" Elisa said.

"Heck, I suppose," Howie said and shrugged.

Frankie said, "More importantly, what do they want?"

"Stevie Brickwald, apparently," C.D. said with some satisfaction.

Danny couldn't see Stevie because he seemed to be buried under a squirming pile of grumbling hounds, but Danny could hear him all right. Stevie was shouting, "Get 'em off me! Get 'em off me!"

Ms. Cosgrove tried to shoo the dogs away, and Elisa cried, *"Gey avec, hundt!"*, which she said always worked on dogs back in Germany, but nothing helped.

"Do something," Ms. Cosgrove shouted at Mr. Hill. Mr. Hill was already pulling at the dogs by their spiked collars, but there were too many of them, and they were too strong.

Chapter Four

Dramatic License or What?

"Shall I save him?" Howie said.

"It would be the right thing to do," Elisa said.

Howie sighed and said, "Very well." He ran forward barking and growling.

By this time, everybody could see that Stevie wasn't actually being hurt by the dogs, and the shrieks of his classmates had turned to laughter and cries of "Oh yuck!"

Two of the Hounds of Heck had their front paws on Stevie Brickwald, and they were taller than he was. They glanced mournfully at Howie, and then went back to poking and tickling Stevie. He put up his arms, attempting to hide from their nosing around.

Howie threw back his head and howled. To Danny, it seemed as if the temperature of the air inside the dome fell to whatever it was outside. The tiny hairs on the back of his neck stood at attention.

Meanwhile, the Hounds of Heck dropped onto

all fours—four legs to a hound—and backed away from Howie. He howled again and they ran off, barking as they had when they first arrived.

Stevie rubbed his eyes with his fists and dragged himself bodily back from the edge of tears. Mr. Hill brushed off his hands and went to comfort him. A moment later Ms. Cosgrove joined them. "Are you all right, Stevie?" she said.

Stevie sniffed and said, "I guess."

"Sure," she said, "you're one tough guy." She glanced at Mr. Hill and said, "That was quite a show, Mr. Hill."

"Er, yes." He didn't look at Ms. Cosgrove.

Ms. Cosgrove said, "I am very impressed by the quality of your special effects. Aren't you, class?"

There was general, if reluctant, agreement.

Howie shook his head at his friends.

"Though perhaps," Ms. Cosgrove went on, "they are a little too realistic."

"I'll say," said Stevie.

"You could be right. I'll look into it." Mr. Hill put his hand on Stevie's shoulder and said, "Will you be all right now?"

"Sure. I ain't afraid of dogs."

"Of course not," Mr. Hill said. He fired up his smile again and said, "Onward to Great Moments in Brooklyn History."

Danny said, "Why do you think Stevie was so popular with the Hounds of Heck?"

"You are complaining?" C.D. said.

"No. Just wondering."

Elisa said, "He is the only child here who is a relative of Overton Hill."

Frankie nodded.

Howie said, "I thought it was his smell that attracted them," and laughed.

They turned off Watling Street onto a side path and came to a big theater front. It was nothing like the gray boxes called theaters that were built in modern shopping malls. Danny had seen ones like it only in old movies and in history books.

It reached into the sky with graceful towers and spires that seemed to soar. And all the soaring parts were decorated with tubes of neon in the shapes of birds' wings and wild fantastic flowers. Big orange letters across the front spelled WONDER HILL BIJOU. Below that, it said NOW PLAYING—GREAT MOMENTS IN BROOKLYN HISTORY. The artificial light under the dome was a little dimmer in this part of the park, giving the neon a chance to show off as it flickered in sequence.

The class walked across the marble forecourt and into the lobby of the theater, where posters in cases decorated with huge plaster leaves advertised wonders of American history miraculously brought to life.

When the class settled in the theater itself, there were plenty of seats left. Smiling, and rubbing his hands together, Roland Hill walked to the front of the room. Like a ringmaster in a circus, he said, "Ladies and gentlemen, boys and girls of all ages, the Wonder Hill Bijou proudly presents Great Moments in Brooklyn History." He felt behind his back, pushed a button and quickly sat down in the front row.

Music began. It was full of horns and violins

and sounded to Danny like the same heroic stuff that came with old pirate movies. Ah well. Mr. Hill had promised Ms. Cosgrove education, and it looked as if he were about to make good his threat.

Light came up on a man dressed kind of like one of the Pilgrims in a Thanksgiving pageant. But he had a wide lace collar, and his boots came up almost to his knees. In a French accent, he said his name was Pierre, and that he was a Walloon from Eastern France. The curtains opened to show more men dressed like him and women in long dresses and head-hugging white caps tied under their chins. The men were cutting down trees and the women were stirring big pots that looked like witches' cauldrons. In the background a dog chased a squirrel around a tree. In 1625, the Walloons were the earliest European settlers in Bruijkleen, what was someday to be Brooklyn.

All the animals and people—even Pierre—were robots, but they were pretty good robots. If Danny kind of squinted he could almost convince himself they were real actors. He rested his head on his fist. He was only moderately interested in Brooklyn's history, and he could tell that most of his classmates were suffering through various stages of boredom. They were eager to go on *real* rides—ones full of thrills and having no educational content whatsoever.

Then a half of the log one of the men had sawed in two rose and floated into the center of the clearing and crashed into the side of a wagon before it fell to the ground. Mr. Hill began to squirm. Danny leaned forward and whispered to C.D., "Is that a special effect or what?"

"It is 'or what,' I believe," C.D. said.

Angela Marconi shushed them, and Danny sat back in his seat a lot more awake than he had been before.

The Walloons slid into the darkness at the back of the stage while British Redcoats and Revolutionary soldiers slid forward. Pierre explained that this was a scene from 1776, the Battle of Long Island, what he called "the first pitched battle of the American Revolution." It was a big victory for the British; Howie cheered when he heard that, and a few of the other kids booed in response. Long rifles flew from the hands of the soldiers and collected themselves in the center of the stage. They began to circle and make flower patterns.

"Are you sure that this is authentic?" Ms. Cosgrove called from the back of the theater.

"Well," Mr. Hill called back, "we take a little dramatic license now and then."

Howie leaned across to Danny and said, "His license should be revoked. I've never heard of rifles dancing during the Revolutionary War."

"Sure," said Danny. "It was the colonists' secret weapon."

Howie chuckled. Danny chuckled too, but he knew Howie was right. Flying logs and dancing rifles weren't the kinds of things anybody would put into a show just to make history more interesting. If the Great Moments in Brooklyn History theater wasn't haunted, Roland Hill had hired some very strange people to design his amusement park.

The soldiers slid into the darkness to be replaced by people in May 1814 boarding the *Nassau*, the first steamboat to cross the East River. That went away to be followed by General Lafayette laying the cornerstone of the first public library in Brooklyn in 1825. Then kids played in a fountain when in 1858, Brooklyn finally had water piped in. The *Monitor*, one of the first ironclad fighting ships, was launched from the Brooklyn Navy Yard in 1862. The climax of the show was the opening of the Brooklyn Bridge on May 24, 1883.

In each scene, something that shouldn't float sailed across the stage. During the opening of the Brooklyn Bridge, the models of the twenty coaches that carried President Chester A. Arthur and his party across the bridge lifted off and dropped into the East River, one coach at a time. It was fascinating to watch.

But the grand finale of the show was a short history of the Hill and Brickwald families, who had lived in Brooklyn nearly from the beginning. Danny couldn't see the real Stevie Brickwald in the audience, but he figured the goon had to be really eating up all this attention.

One of the robots was a representation of Overton Hill, who used to own most of the land on which Wonder Hill now stood. If the robot was accurate, Overton had been a tall thin man, with a nose like a buggy whip and feet like shovels. Under his arm he carried a ledger—a big book in which he kept track of who owed him money—and he had a very serious look on his face. Danny wondered if in real life that serious look hadn't been a sour sneer. People don't curse other people for nothing. Danny didn't see anyone who looked like the man who'd done the actual cursing.

The latest in the long line of Hills and Brickwalds was Stevie Brickwald himself. Like the other robots, he slid into the light on a platform that thrust forward from the darkness at the back of the stage. Danny studied the robot of Stevie critically. It looked kind of like Stevie, but the sculptor hadn't quite captured Stevie's nasty grin.

Overton Hill slid forward. Danny didn't think much of that. Robots had been sliding across the stage all through the show. Then Danny noticed that Overton's feet were nowhere near the ground. He wasn't sliding. He was floating. Danny got cold all over and his skin prickled. Overton floated in front of the other Hills and Danny could see right through him. If that was a special effect, it was a good one.

As Overton Hill approached the robot of Stevie Brickwald, the robot saw him coming and backed off, crying, "Get away from me, you *thing*!" Danny suddenly realized that it was no robot, but the real Stevie up there.

Somebody a few rows in front of Danny and to one side began to whimper. Jason Nickles cried out, "Look out, Stevie!" Most of the kids didn't say anything. They barely moved, too petrified with fear by the unscheduled excitement.

But Overton came at Stevie, one long knobby hand reaching out like the branch of a bare tree, the other hand clutching his ledger. Stevie backed as Overton Hill advanced. "Do something, Uncle Roland," Stevie shouted.

But Uncle Roland was in no shape to do anything. He had collapsed into his seat and was watching the spectacle on stage through his fingers.

Stevie backed into a robot of one of his ancestors, the one wearing a cowboy outfit. Launching sparks, the cowboy fell into a woman wearing a wide white dress that looked as if it were made of birthday cake. She shot off sparks too as she fell against a man wearing a bowler and a tight-fitting suit. Robots were falling down all over the stage now, each of them spouting sparks.

Overton grabbed Stevie's collar and cried, "The hounds were right! This is a relative! An innocent child! I am saved!" Either by design or by accident, Stevie shook free of Overton and leaped off the stage. Overton put his fingers to his mouth and made a shrill whistle.

Stevie got about halfway up the aisle to the exit when Danny heard the baying of dogs. Stevie froze and looked around, confused. The Hounds of Heck were racing down the aisle. Overton was behind them, pointing at Stevie, urging the hounds on. Stevie ran back down the aisle and through a door next to the stage that said WONDER WORKERS ONLY. The door shut behind him on a spring.

The hounds were not bothered by the door. They ran through it as if it were not there, chasing Stevie as if he were a squirrel. Overton floated

after them, waving his ledger and crying, "He must not escape!" He went through the closed door too.

The theater was quiet but for the sputtering of sparks and the crying and shrieking of Danny's higher strung classmates.

Chapter Five

Stevie's Comin'
'Round the Mountain
When He Comes

Ms. Cosgrove ran to the front of the theater and shouted, "It's all right, class." Then she shook Mr. Hill, trying to get him to stand up and do something. But Mr. Hill kept his head in his hands and he refused to look up.

Danny saw Elisa and Frankie climb over seats to get to the aisle. They made their way through the noisy mob Ms. Cosgrove's class had become and stood at the door through which Stevie had been pursued. In an instant, they were joined by C.D. "Come on," Danny said, motioning to Howie.

"Please get back to your seats," Ms. Cosgrove shouted after them, but then she was occupied comforting a shrieking Marla Willaby.

Danny and the others pushed open the heavy door and stood at the end of a short white corridor. Cables and pipes ran along the ceiling. Gray boxes with blinking red lights were attached to the walls. Beyond the door at the other end of the corridor the hounds were still baying, and Howie guessed that they hadn't caught Stevie yet.

"What do we do now?" Danny said.

"We save him," Elisa said.

"That would certainly be sporting of us," Howie said without enthusiasm.

"It is the second time," C.D. intoned.

"Maybe," said Danny, "if we save Stevie again, he'll leave us alone."

"You believe this?" Frankie said.

His sister shrugged. "There is an easy way to find out if it will happen."

"Besides," said Danny, "if we don't stop Overton Hill from haunting this place, it'll never open and nobody'll ever be able to come here again."

They walked to the end of the corridor, opened the door, and went down three cement stairs into a big room. Like shelves in a library, tall frames of wires and relays crossed the room, row on row. The howling of the hounds was louder here but it could not drown out the electric hum.

"Ah," said Frankie. "The brain of Great Moments in Brooklyn History."

"What means this?" C.D. said.

"This is the control room for all robots and special effects."

"I see."

Elisa led the way between the electronic frames. Near the other end of the room Stevie ran across their path like a figure in a shooting gallery.

"Come on," Howie said, pushing his way past Elisa and Frankie. He ran to where Stevie had disappeared around a corner and looked both ways before turning right.

At that moment the baying of the hounds suddenly became louder, and the pack was bearing down upon them. Overton Hill flew like a bad thought over the hounds crying, "Find him!" The kids began to run, but the hounds were too fast. Just when Danny thought he and the others were going to be trampled under dozens of heavy paws, the hounds ran right through them. As it happened, Danny felt a whisper of a sensation in his belly, like when he wanted to burp but couldn't. The feeling was gone with the hounds.

At the other end of the row the dogs sniffed the floor, then bounded off to the right.

The kids followed as quietly as they could. Overton Hill was still urging on his hounds, and the hounds were still baying. The sound got farther away.

"Here they are," Danny whispered.

Howie was standing with two Stevies. One of them looked nervous and wild-eyed. The other one seemed to be asleep. The sleeping one wore a Wonder Hill sweatshirt.

"Are they gone?" Stevie said.

"For the moment," Howie said. "I circled around a bit to throw them off Stevie's scent."

"They will be back," C.D. said. In his Transylvanian accent, the prediction sounded ominous.

"Who's your friend?" Danny asked, pointing to the sleeping Stevie.

The awake Stevie glowered while Frankie answered, "It must be the Stevie robot that would normally be used in the last scene of Great Moments in Brooklyn History.

44

"It's a great robot," Stevie bragged. "But the real thing is even better, huh? Uncle Roland lets me do whatever I want so I went on stage instead."

Danny said, "I guess your uncle Roland didn't expect Wonder Hill to be quite so haunted."

"That robot gives me an idea, old chaps," Howie said. "Frankie, can you get it going?"

"I will look," Frankie said. He opened the back of the robot Stevie and poked around, reminding Danny of a doctor examining a patient.

"Hurry up," Stevie complained. "I've never seen such slow monsters."

Frankie ignored him and continued his examination. When he was done, he nodded and closed up the robot. "Anytime," he said.

"Right now," said Howie. "Send him in that direction." He pointed away from the door through which they'd come in.

"This better work," Stevie wailed, still trying to act tough but having a hard time of it.

Elisa said, "Nothing will work if you continue to announce our presence here."

Stevie opened his mouth to say something, but shrank into himself and stayed quiet.

Frankie asked for Elisa's help. She put her hands flat on the robot's chest and Frankie put his hands around its head. There was a crackle of electricity and the robot jumped. It opened its eyes and slowly turned around.

"It is not very smart," Frankie said.

Stevie angrily showed his fist to Frankie. Frankie pushed him away with a short zap of electricity. Stevie jumped back and put his fist down, but he was still angry.

45

"We are trying to help you," C.D. said.

"Then *help* me, already."

Frankie lifted the robot and turned it to face the right way. He put one hand around its neck and gave it one more shot of electricity. It walked away a little wobbly, but at the moment the real Stevie was a little wobbly too.

The kids moved as quickly as possible to the end of the frame. Howie turned the corner and stopped, surprised and horrified. The voice of Overton Hill came to Danny: "Welcome, children."

"That's him," Stevie cried and ran off again. Overton Hill and his hounds didn't waste time before running after him.

Frankie said, "Stevie has no maneuvering room. They will catch him this time."

Still, the kids followed the action. They stopped when the baying of the hounds suddenly stopped, then ran until they came to a door with an Exit sign glowing red over it.

Howie swung the door open. Danny and the others crowded out after him and stood outside the theater at the bottom of a ramp that lead back into the park. It was the only way Stevie could have gone. Danny could still hear the baying of dogs in the distance.

Howie sniffed the air and turned his head, getting his bearings. He cried, "Once more into the breach, dear friends," and ran off.

"He means what?" C.D. said.

"I don't know, but I'm not waiting here," Danny said, and ran after Howie. A bat flew by over his head, and he knew C.D. was on the trail. "Wait for us," Frankie called. For all his strength and size, he was not much of a runner. Elisa always kept him company.

They passed among beautiful landscaped gardens, each with its tiny cement elves sitting on tiny cement mushrooms. Danny almost stopped to see if a wishing well worked, but he didn't want to lose sight of Howie, who moved awfully fast.

They ran between Titania's Jewelry Shoppe and Ye Olde Woodcutter, and crossed Watling Street. Towering behind the thatched cottages was Fairy's Flight, the roller coaster.

Danny froze when he heard Howie's werewolf howl. Howie was not far away. Elisa shouted, "We must hurry," as she passed Danny with Frankie.

Danny and the others caught up with Howie and C.D. at the foot of Fairy's Flight mountain. Howie was panting like a dog. C.D. was sucking on his Fluid of Life. They were both looking up the mountain.

"Aaiiee!" came an echoing cry. Almost at the top of the mountain, flashes of Stevie—gripping the front rail, his mouth open wide—could be seen as he zoomed along ledges in a Fairy's Flight roller coaster car and then dived out of sight.

"Look," said Howie. He wasn't pointing at Stevie or even where Stevie had been, but at the sides of the big artificial mountain. There, among the miniature waterfalls, painted snow, and fake pine trees were the Hounds of Heck, speeding up the side of the mountain as if they were moving across flat ground.

"Come on," Danny said, leading them around the mountain to the place where the ride ended.

Hundreds of Fairy's Flight cars were lined up on a side track, each with its fairy light bobbing at the tip of a stiff wire that arched from the front. Stevie continued to yell—whether because the ride was exciting or because the Hounds of Heck were doing something unspeakable to him, Danny didn't know. He was nervous about finding out.

Nearly at the bottom, Stevie's car went by with a whoosh and a roar. Big autumn-colored things were in the car with him. On the next pass, the car glided around the side of the mountain at ground level and screeched as the brakes in the track slowed it. Stevie was trying to protect himself with his arms while two hounds, one on either side, were licking him with their big slobbery tongues.

"He's drowning in dog spit," Danny said.

Elisa said, "As your sister Barbara would say— 'yuckers.' "

"Do it, Howie," C.D. said.

Howie nodded, said, "Right," then lifted his voice into a howl. It was a howl to freeze water, a howl to frighten cement. It was a howl that should have sent the Hounds of Heck whence they came. And it did, so to speak.

The problem was that before they left, one of the hounds grabbed Stevie by the shirt collar with its mouth and picked him up. He yowled and waved his arms. Nothing impressed the hound. It ran off with the rest of the pack, carrying Stevie as if he were a kitten.

Chapter Six

Oops!

"Come on, C.D.," Howie said. He closed his eyes, and his nose lengthened into a stubby black pug as his hair grew out so fast Danny could actually see it spreading across his arms and down his forehead. Howie howled and ran after the hounds on his hands and knuckles.

C.D. said, "We five will meet again at Great Moments in Brooklyn History." He leaped into the air and became a bat. The bat circled Danny and the Stein kids once and flew after Howie.

Danny said, "I guess we should go see how Ms. Cosgrove is doing."

"Yes," said Frankie. "Perhaps Mr. Hill is rational again and can tell us more about Overton Hill."

They walked briskly across Watling Street and this time Danny did stop at the wishing well. He threw in a dime and said, "I wish everything will turn out OK."

Elisa agreed that that seemed to cover the entire situation. Frankie looked into the well, but made no comment.

When they got there, the Great Moments in Brooklyn History theater was empty. A strange electric smell was in the air. Frankie identified it as ozone. Black thready smoke rose from some of the robots that were still lying on stage, but Ms. Cosgrove and her class, even Mr. Hill, were gone.

"This is very spooky," Danny said.

"There is a scientific explanation," Frankie said, but he didn't sound certain.

"We will wait," Elisa said.

That seemed like a good idea to Danny and Frankie too. While Elisa and Danny sat on the lip of the stage swinging their legs, Frankie strolled around the stage, studying the damaged robots. He made little comments and thinking noises to himself.

Against his will, Danny found himself imagining that things he couldn't see were sitting in all the theater seats. If he could see them, he wouldn't want to see them. They had tentacles and drippy faces and stingers and claws. Something in one of the robots popped, and he and Elisa jumped. Frankie just clucked.

Elisa said, "Frankie can repair anything that has a wiring diagram."

"Too bad our problem is supernatural instead of electronic," Danny said.

"Yes," Elisa said.

Soon, they heard noise outside and they leaped to the floor. Frankie carefully jumped down next to them. The noise didn't sound like Hounds of

Heck, and indeed it wasn't. It was Mr. Hill and Ms. Cosgrove and the rest of their class.

"Where have you been?" said Ms. Cosgrove. Her hair was all mussed, and she had the wild eyes of someone who had been shopping in crowds all day. Her voice was a little frantic. "Where are Howie and C.D.?"

"Looking for Stevie," Elisa said.

"He's in no danger, I assure you," Mr. Hill said.

Ms. Cosgrove said, "I suppose Stevie was in on this little drama right from the beginning."

"Almost."

"Well, from now on, I want everyone to stay together till Mr. Hill can fix his machinery."

"Fix?" said Frankie.

"Yes. He assures me that Stevie is fine. The special effects just got out of hand. Isn't that right, Mr. Hill?"

"A new operation always needs a little fine tuning," Mr. Hill said.

"That is true," Frankie said.

Jason Nickles said, "We couldn't leave even if Stevie was here. The doors are locked."

"Not locked," Mr. Hill said. "Merely blocked by snow."

Ms. Cosgrove said, "That is one more thing you'll have to fix, isn't it, Mr. Hill?"

Mr. Hill smiled and said, "Yes, of course."

Ms. Cosgrove looked around and said, "Is there a telephone, Mr. Hill?"

"Certainly. The park is fully equipped." They walked down the aisle to the front of the theater, where Ms. Cosgrove and Mr. Hill pushed through a door that said WONDER WORKERS ONLY.

Danny spoke quietly to Frankie and Elisa. He said, "I don't think Mr. Hill knows any more about what's going on than we do."

"Less," said Frankie.

"One thing is certain," said Elisa. "Finding Overton Hill and Stevie is the key to escaping from Wonder Hill."

"Escaping?" Danny said. "You think Overton Hill locked the doors?"

Elisa shrugged. "I do not know. But it is logical to assume that Overton's ghost is responsible for the problems at Wonder Hill."

A moment later, Ms. Cosgrove and Mr. Hill returned, staring at the floor and looking worried. "Please sit down, class," Ms. Cosgrove said gravely. Danny had not seen her so upset since her Parents' Night model of P.S. 13 had been stolen. The class caught her mood, and they found seats with a minimum of fuss.

Ms. Cosgrove said, "The phones are dead. The doors are locked." She looked at Mr. Hill. "Or at least jammed. We'll just have to sit tight for now."

"There is plenty of food, bathrooms, fresh air," Mr. Hill said gaily.

"We'll be fine," Ms. Cosgrove said.

Angela Marconi said confidently, "My father is a pillar of the community. He won't like it that I'm stuck here."

"Hey," said Mr. Hill. "It's only temporary."

Some of the kids looked as if they were in shock. Others began to discuss the problem among themselves. Mr. Hill sat in a chair while Ms.

Cosgrove moved around the room, laughing and making jokes with her students. Her smile looked almost real. Danny was impressed with how she was handling the situation.

Elisa nodded to Frankie and Danny, and they walked to where Mr. Hill was sitting. Mr. Hill looked up at them and attempted a smile. He wasn't as good at it as Ms. Cosgrove. "What is it, kids?"

"We have important questions," Elisa said.

"Why should you be any different?" He shook his head. "What are they?"

Elisa said, "Why did you invite us here if you knew Wonder Hill was haunted?"

Mr. Hill looked surprised, then he got cagey, the way adults sometimes get when they think they can bluff a child. He said, "What makes you think the place is haunted?"

"I know much about special effects," Frankie said. "What we have seen cannot be explained by them."

"I suppose not," Mr. Hill said, and formed his lips around a silent whistle as he thought. At last he said, "So what if the place is haunted? The ghost never actually hurt anybody."

"We are locked in," Elisa said.

Mr. Hill shook his head and said, "It's the snow."

"Maybe," said Danny. "What about Stevie?"

Mr. Hill looked at the floor as he thought some more. Then he looked up at the kids and said, "All right. How much do you know?"

Danny said, "We know that the ghost who controls the Hounds of Heck and who captured Stevie is Overton Hill."

Elisa said, "We know also that he has been cursed. We suspect that is why he is haunting your amusement park."

"Cursed?" Mr. Hill said, surprised.

"You didn't know about that?" Danny said.

"No." Mr. Hill looked around. Ms. Cosgrove was on the other side of the room, still ministering to the shocked and frightened. Mr. Hill said, "Look, you kids seem bright. And I guess you know more about this than I do, though I don't know how."

"We held a seance," Elisa said.

Mr. Hill's eyes got big, and he nodded. He said, "That would do it, I guess. Anyway, I invited the class to Wonder Hill hoping the innocent laughter of children would be stronger than the ghost's power. I guess it didn't work."

"Do not give up so easily," said Elisa.

"No?" said Mr. Hill hopefully.

Elisa nodded to Mr. Hill, then to Frankie and Danny. The three kids saw that Ms. Cosgrove was still busy, and they backed out between the exit curtains. They hurried down the ramp and around to the front of Great Moments in Brooklyn History where they waited for Howie and C.D.

While they stood there, Danny became aware of the constant hiss of the air conditioning. Then, he became aware of faraway moaning and creaking. Danny knew it was only the giant dome moving in the wind and straining under tons of snow, but the sound was ghostly. These small lonely noises made Wonder Hill seem to be on another planet.

Then a bat flapped into sight with a werewolf running not far behind him. The bat turned into C.D. and began to suck Fluid of Life. The werewolf changed into Howie. He said, "Sorry, chums," curled up on a bench and went to sleep.

"Did you find them?" Danny said.

"We did not. Hounds of Heck are very fast and they know the park better than we. You discovered what?"

Elisa said, "Only that Mr. Hill knew Wonder Hill was haunted. He claims not to know about the curse."

"Also," said Frankie, "the doors cannot be opened and the telephones do not work."

"Americans have a word for this," said C.D. "I believe it is 'oops.' "

"You got that right," said Danny.

"We must get out of this place," Elisa said. "And we cannot do that without confronting Overton Hill's ghost and finding out why he kidnapped Stevie."

"And rescuing Stevie in the process," Danny added.

Elisa nodded. "It is right that we do so. Stevie is no friend to us, but even he does not deserve to be captive to the Hounds of Heck."

Howie yawned and sat up. "What did I miss?" he said.

C.D. said, "We are locked in. The telephones do not work. We must rescue Stevie or remain prisoners."

"Rum go," Howie said. "But we must keep a stiff upper lip."

"Stiff lips," C.D. said, agreeing.

"I have an idea," Danny said.

"Jolly good. Let's have it."

"Maybe we can still get the Hounds of Heck to lead us to Stevie and Overton Hill."

"How?" said C.D.

"Maybe instead of scaring the Hounds of Heck, Howie can make friends with them. He can call them here and then send them home. Maybe if they aren't in so much of a hurry, we'll be able to keep up with them."

"Ripping."

"You can do this, Howie?" Elisa said.

"Unquestionably. Give me room."

The other kids backed off and Howie gathered himself together. When he howled, Danny noticed the difference right away. This was a more natural howl than the type Howie normally produced. It sounded lonely, like a coyote far out in the desert, instead of something that could wilt aluminum. Howie put some yips at the end of it, which was a nice touch. But nothing happened.

"Try again," Elisa said.

Howie tried again, howling a medley of barks, yips, and downright shouts. Danny said, "Does that mean something?"

Howie said, "It's the doggie version of 'come 'round sometime for a visit.' "

Howie was about to try for a third time when Danny and the others heard the baying of big dogs. The kids planted their feet more firmly. Danny told himself he was ready for anything.

The hounds arrived leaping over one another like puppies, their tongues lolling from their mouths. They gathered around, sniffing and leaping and licking at Danny and the Stein kids. The hounds' breath had not improved. Danny got the worst of it because he was shorter than the others. Being licked across the face by their enormous sloppy tongues was like being kissed by wet dishrags.

Howie whined a little at the hounds in dog talk and pointed across the park. They seemed to understand because they whined back and trotted in the direction from which they'd come.

"Step lively, now," said Howie, and lit out after them.

Even though the Hounds of Heck were only trotting, the kids had difficulty keeping up. The main problem was not so much their speed—though that was considerable—as the fact that they could go through things the kids had to go around. The wishing well, being so small, wasn't much of a problem, but the hounds could go through the walls of the shops on Watling Street, and the kids lost sight of them. After running around Cobweb's Candy Kitchen to the street itself, Danny said, "There they are!" The hounds were streaming up Watling Street toward Stonehenge.

The kids followed, Howie in the lead. They hurried across the open space inside the circle of giant stone posts and lintels of Stonehenge. Danny knew it was no more real than anything else at Wonder Hill, but he had the feeling that ancient Druids were watching him while they waited for midsummer's morn, when the sun would rise over one particular stone in the circle.

Just beyond was Yggdrasil. Its trunk was bigger around than a house, and its massive knotted branches, each thick enough to support elephants, twisted as they reached for the roof of the Wonder Hill dome. Roots clawed into the earth like the fingers of giants. The hounds went right through the tree as if it were so much smoke. As the kids circled the tree, Frankie tapped the bark and announced that it was made from some kind of plastic.

Yggdrasil marked the entrance to a dim forest. The trees were real, but sitting in their branches were mechanical animals that called down to the kids, "Climb the glass mountain," and, "The old beggar is more than he seems," and, "Plant the magic beans outside your window in the moonlight."

"Good advice for somebody," C.D. said.

"Fairy-tale characters," Elisa said.

"Kiss me. I'm really a prince," said a mechanical frog sitting on a lily pad in the middle of a pond.

To get across the pond the kids had to use a wooden bridge that seemed as if it were about to fall apart.

"It must be stronger than it looks," Frankie said.

"It must," Danny said.

Howie said, "We are in an amusement park, not running an obstacle course." He strode confidently out onto the bridge, and it held his weight. When he was about halfway across, an ugly creature rose from the water until its shoulders were clear. It had long stringy black hair and a big flat nose, and its face was marked with small arrows and stars and moons. Its earlobes hung to the water. In a terrible voice that made trucks changing gears sound like music, it said, "Pay the troll."

"Of course," said Danny, "it's a troll bridge."

"We have nothing to pay him with," C.D. said.

"It's an amusement park," said Howie again. "We don't have to pay him." He walked to the other side of the bridge and the troll sank back into the water. They waited a moment and nothing happened.

As each of them crossed, the troll rose from the water again and made its demand, but that's all he did.

"Not a very successful troll, is he?" Danny said.

"Maybe he's just shy," Howie said.

Through the trees, Danny could see Adventure Court, an open area paved with stone surrounded by low buildings, where there were more rides. At last the kids were in the open again, and Danny saw the Hounds of Heck gliding across a lake as if they were ice skating.

"Chivalry Lake," Howie said as the kids came to the edge of the land. He was the only one who was not out of breath.

"There they go," said Danny, gasping. The Hounds of Heck were clambering up onto the grassy bank of an island in the center of Chivalry Lake. Studying a map fastened to the stump of a tree, Elisa said, "The island is Avalon, supposedly King Arthur's final resting place."

The hounds trotted along a path and skated across a moat, continued through a raised drawbridge into a tall gray castle. Colorful pennants at

59

the top of each turret fluttered and snapped in the air-conditioning.

"Well," said Howie. "Have they gone through the castle, or is it their destination?"

"We are near the edge of the park."

"Frankie is right," Elisa said. "Unless they went outside, they have gone no farther."

Danny said, "If Overton Hill is haunting the park, probably the Hounds of Heck are too."

"There you are then," Howie said. "Shall we swim for it?"

"We will not have to," C.D. said. He pointed. An empty rowboat was sailing into view around one end of Avalon. At ground level there was nothing but the gentlest breeze, but the rowboat floated toward them without hesitation. They watched, fascinated, as it slid into the bank at their feet and bumped gently.

"It is a sign," C.D. said.

"It's an invitation," Howie said, "that's for sure. The question is, do we accept?"

Chapter Seven

The Terrible Toomler

Danny gulped and said, "I don't think we can *not* accept."

"Danny is right," Elisa said.

"Besides," said Howie, "we didn't come all this way to quit now. We must carry on." He stepped into the rowboat, making it rock a little. He turned to look at them, but nobody moved. "Come on, then." Howie held out his hands to Elisa. She stepped carefully into the boat, making it rock more. C.D. leaped lightly and sat down in the stern. Danny came next. Frankie mournfully looked at his friends in the boat. "I will stay here," he said. "I will defend our rear."

"Don't be silly, old man," Howie said. "Our rear is fine." He and Elisa both held out their hands. Frankie stepped into the boat with one foot, and did a split as it slid away from the shore. "Heave now, Elisa," Howie said, and they pulled Frankie into the boat. He fell in the bottom between the seats.

"Am I drowned?" he said.

"Nothing like it, old man," Howie said.

Frankie sat up and looked around. "We are not moving," he said.

"And there are no paddles," C.D. said.

"No oars, anyway," Howie agreed.

Danny said a long "Ah," as if he suddenly understood when the boat moved away from the bank by itself.

"Brilliant," said Howie happily. "Our problem is solved."

"Yeah," said Danny. "I wonder how many miles we get to the ghost."

They glided smoothly across the water. It would have been a pleasant trip for Danny if he hadn't been worrying so much about what they'd find inside the castle. The others seemed pretty tense too. Even Howie.

The rowboat came up parallel with the grassy bank of Avalon, and Howie leaped out to help the others onto land. Frankie was the last again. He licked his lips and jumped, lost his balance and rolled over onto the grass. He wasn't graceful, but his acrobatics got the job done. He stood up and joined the other kids at the end of the path that led to the drawbridge.

They marched forward, Danny and Howie and C.D. in the front rank, Frankie and Elisa defending the rear. Although, as Howie had pointed out, it was unlikely an attack would come from that direction.

Danny felt as if he were approaching the throne of the Wizard of Oz, but it was too much to hope that they would find a funny little man behind a curtain who was responsible for Overton Hill's

curse and for the doors being locked and the phones being broken. The only wizard in the place was Roland Hill, and he knew less about what was going on than they did.

The drawbridge creaked as it lowered on heavy metal chains, and it was all the way down by the time they reached it. Without hesitating, they walked across the wooden planks and into the cool dim interior of the castle.

There were picture windows in the rugged stone walls of the entryway, and each one showed King Arthur at a different time in his life. Normally, that would have been just the sort of thing that would interest Danny, but at the moment he had other things on his mind.

The corridor ended in a big room with a high ceiling and banners hung in rows along the walls. Each banner showed a pattern of mythical animals or crowns or swords, and Danny knew that each pattern would identify a different knight. In niches below the flags were suits of armor. Electric torches, like the ones in Oberon's Hall, flickered between the niches.

"There's Arthur's throne," Howie whispered, nodding at the biggest of the chairs pulled up to round table that filled the center of the room.

From the depths of the castle came the whine of Stevie Brickwald's voice. "I'm finished," he said.

"No, no," came a man's voice. "More fun to come."

A single Hound of Heck walked into the throne room and made one explosive woof. He walked away, then turned to look at them. "Very well," said Howie. Howie walked toward the hound, and it turned away again. It led Howie and the others along another corridor, past bathrooms, and into a small stone room with a high vaulted ceiling. Yellow light fell like a wedge of cheese through a narrow window in one wall.

The Hound of Heck hurrumphed as it flopped onto the floor where the other hounds were already scattered like lumpy throw rugs. It rested its muzzle on the cold stones and moved its eyes from the kids to Overton Hill.

Overton Hill was sitting on a stool behind a high slim desk, scratching in his ledger with a big feather pen. His knees were drawn up nearly to his chin, and his legs made Danny think of chicken wings. Nearby, at a long wooden table laden with gold coins, sat Stevie. He had been stacking the coins in columns of ten in a row in front of him. He stopped now, and as he looked at the monster kids he smiled. "Am I glad to see you guys," he said.

"Stevie?" said Elisa in disbelief.

"Perhaps he's been enchanted," said Howie.

"Not enchanted," Stevie said. "Just bored out of my gourd. Can you guys break me out of here?"

Overton Hill was looking at them and nodding. He was a grim man, and the smile matched his general attitude. He said, "The more the merrier," and cackled as he leaped from his stool. Danny could see through him to the stool and the desk and wall as if Overton Hill were a lace window curtain.

Overton Hill put his arms around the shoulders

of Howie and Danny. The arm around Danny's shoulder had no weight, but it was a definite pressure. It forced him forward and down onto a bench at the table with Stevie. "The rest of you too," said Overton Hill. "No dawdling."

When everybody was settled, Overton Hill once again said, "The more the merrier," and waved his hand at the table. A pile of gold coins appeared in front of each of them. The coins were as transparent as Overton Hill himself. Ghost coins, Danny thought.

"Count now," said Overton Hill.

"Count who?" C.D. said.

"Not who," Overton Hill said, "but what. I want ten coins to a stack." He scrambled back up his stool like a lizard and smiled at them unpleasantly. "Count smartly now, or I'll have the hounds on you." He began to scribble in his ledger again.

"What's going on?" Danny whispered to Stevie.

Stevie shrugged and shook his head. "I don't know. Every time I finish counting the coins I have, he waves his hand and makes some more." He poked a stack of coins with one finger. They fell into a long low staircase.

"But why?" Frankie said. He studied one coin closely.

"He keeps talking about fun," Stevie said.

"No whispering there," cried Overton Hill. "Count ten coins to a stack, five stacks to a row."

"But why?" said Elisa out loud as she moved some coins around.

"Why?" said Overton Hill as if he could not believe anyone could be so dense.

"Yes," said Elisa. "Why?"

Overton Hill leaped from his stool and floated to the floor. "Why? Because it is fun, that's why. In life I ran a counting house, and I had no greater joy than to total up my accounts and see how much money I had collected."

"A thin sort of joy," Howie said.

"It was all I cared for. Now count." He pointed at them sternly.

"But it is not fun for us," Elisa said.

"Impossible," Overton Hill said, and with a pop no louder than that made by a bursting soap bubble, he was back behind his desk, scratching madly with his pen.

"But—" said C.D.

Elisa interrupted. "We will count," she said loudly. In a much softer voice, she said, "We must discover the reason Overton Hill wants us to have fun."

"He is a toomler," Frankie said. He set one coin atop another, then a third atop the first two.

"What's a toomler?" Danny said.

Elisa said, "It is what in the Old Country we call a professional merrymaker. He makes sure everybody at a party or on vacation has a good time."

Danny grumbled, "He's a terrible toomler, if that's what he is."

There was agreement around the table, even from Stevie. As a matter of fact, Danny decided he liked Stevie a lot more when he was in trouble and on unfamiliar territory. Since Danny and his friends had come into the room, Stevie had been agreeable and pleasant—astonishing, but there it was.

Suddenly, Frankie pushed his pile of coins away and said loudly, "This is not logical."

"None of that now," Overton Hill said as he flicked his pen in their direction. "The sooner you start having fun, the better I'll like it."

Elisa folded her hands. "This is not fun," she said.

"Bosh," said Overton Hill. "Children don't know what fun is."

"We know it when we see it," Danny said. "And this isn't it."

"Why would we lie?" said Howie.

"Why indeed?" said Overton Hill as he tapped the feather end of his pen against his lips.

Stevie Brickwald said, "If I was having fun, I'd tell you. Really." He and C.D. nodded at each other.

Overton Hill studied them as if he could see lies on their faces, plain as dirt. The grimness in his face melted into sadness. His lower lip trembled. In the quiet of the room Danny could hear the hounds growling softly. Overton Hill folded his arms across his desk and lowered his head onto them. In a voice muffled by his arms, he said, "No wonder this never works. I am cursed till I am generous with my fun. I am doomed."

"Perhaps," C.D. said, "the curse could be lifted."

"No, no," Overton Hill said into his arms.

"There is another way," said Elisa. "An easier way."

"Indeed," said Howie. "The man is starving at a banquet."

"We'll show you fun," said Danny.

Chapter Eight

If You Knew Heinrick Like I Know Heinrick

"No, no," said Overton Hill. "It is useless. For hundreds of years it has been useless." He looked up at them with his red-rimmed eyes and said, "I have not the same idea of fun as most others. I could not reform if I wanted to."

"Nonsense," said C.D. "My family has much experience with curses. They come. They go. A curse one person can invoke is a curse another person can break."

"So say you."

"So say us all," C.D. said and wrapped his cape around himself.

"You don't know Heinrick van Donk," Overton Hill said, and shuddered. "One who is cursed by him, stays cursed."

"We met him," Howie said. "He is not as tough as he seems."

"Met him? How?"

"We had a seance," Danny said.

"What, pray tell, is a seance?"

69

"It is a summoning of ghosts and spirits," Howie said. "Elisa is our medium."

"Still, you don't know Heinrick like I do."

Elisa said, "You are right. But think: If the curse laid down by Heinrick van Donk cannot be lifted, it certainly can be broken. All you must do is be generous with your fun. It is what you said yourself."

"I don't know what other people think is fun," Overton Hill wailed.

"We will show you," C.D. said, and snapped his cape open. Overton Hill peered at him as if he expected the answer to his problem was written on C.D.'s shirtfront. When he didn't find it there, he looked at the intense, serious faces of the kids. "Dare I hope?" he said.

"Why not?" Danny said.

"Sure," said Stevie. "You couldn't be any worse off than you are now."

A wild smile spread across Overton Hill's face. Danny did not like it any more than the grim variety. Overton Hill said, "I believe you're right. What do you suggest?"

"This is an amusement park," Elisa said. "Let us amuse ourselves."

"So," said Overton Hill astonished, "that is what it is. In my time, amusement came in other forms."

Stevie said, "My uncle Roland Hill built this place. Every ride we go on will be fun."

"Then we will go on rides," Overton Hill said. He put his fingers to his mouth and whistled as he had back at Great Moments in Brooklyn History. The Hounds of Heck climbed to their feet and shook themselves. "Fun," Overton Hill cried. "Amusement! Onward!" The hounds pushed the kids with their cold potato noses.

"Hey," shouted Stevie and resisted.

"Come on, Stevie," Danny said, and dragged him out of the room after the monster kids. The Hounds of Heck pursued the kids through King Arthur's throne room and out of the castle. The kids stampeded across the drawbridge and down the grassy bank where they lost no time getting aboard the boat. With its nose high in the air, it skimmed like a shot back to the mainland. The Hounds of Heck skated alongside them. Over all this activity, Overton Hill floated, driving them on. "Fun," he cried. "More fun! Faster! Faster!"

"Gnome Caverns," shouted C.D. He led the way to an entrance that let them into a low tunnel lit by small red lamps. Danny heard deep voices singing a strange work song. But he had no time to enjoy wondering who might be singing before the hounds were urging him deeper into the earth, past tunnels where mechanical gnomes used picks and shovels to uncover glittering diamonds which other gnomes loaded onto carts and more gnomes pushed away on tracks. They sang as they worked.

There were a lot of galleries and tunnels Danny and the others could have explored, but the hounds never stopped pushing them. The kids were forced to clamber into mining cars like the ones the gnomes used and ride back to the surface. Overton Hill called down to them, "Are you having fun yet?"

"Almost," Danny shouted back. "But—"

"But no buts, my boy! Fun awaits you!"

If the kids were not to drown in dog spit or be poked black and blue, they had to hurry on to Jack's Beanstalk, a tall thin parachute ride.

"I don't want to go up there," Stevie said, pulling back.

"You'll not deny yourself the fun," Overton Hill cried, and the hounds forced them into a bean-pod car barely large enough to hold all six of them. Stevie's eyes were big and frightened, and he gripped the handrail as the car rose quickly. Danny could sympathize. They were a long way from the ground, and he knew what was coming next.

The car reached the top and stopped for a second before a parachute opened above them, and the car dropped. Danny's stomach was left behind. Everybody yelled as the ground rushed up at them, but the parachute slowed them just in time. The bean-pod car door opened, and they staggered from it weak-kneed but unharmed.

"Enough of this noise," Stevie said. "Ol' Great-grandpa Overton can haunt this place all he wants." Stevie stalked away, but hounds headed him off and herded him back to the group, which was already on its way to the Cooper Works Bumper Barrels.

Danny wanted to tell Overton Hill that this was no way to have fun, but he was still winded from the beanstalk ride, and the hounds would not let him stop to catch his breath. Besides, it looked to Danny as if Overton Hill had been driven a little crazy by his long haunt of the ground on which Wonder Hill now stood. Anybody in his or her right mind could have seen the kids were not having a good time and would continue not having a good time as long as they were pushed around the way the hounds were doing. Overton Hill just wasn't paying attention.

The hounds ran the kids out onto the bumper barrel stage, and then separated each of them into a plastic barrel that had a metal bumper all around it. While each of the kids was in a barrel, a bell rang and the cars began to move.

"This is more like it," Stevie said. Then Danny was too occupied steering his own barrel to follow what anybody else was doing. He was in no mood to ram anybody and he didn't think his monster friends were either, but the barrels scurried so fast, he could not help himself. He gave a yell and took one teeth-jarring bump after another.

The bell rang again, but the barrels did not stop—they just went faster, throwing Danny from side to side so hard his shoulders hurt. Danny didn't know how he was doing it, but Overton Hill obviously had taken control of the bumper barrels. He could probably control any ride he wanted to just by haunting it and make it go on as long as he wanted it too. The barrels went faster yet, and if it hadn't been for the safety belt, Danny would have been thrown from the barrel like a cannonball from a cannon.

"This isn't fun," Danny cried, feeling as if he were a milk shake. But with the noise of the shouting and of the wind, and of the bumper barrels rolling and bumping, he could barely hear the words himself.

When the barrels finally slowed to a stop, Danny was torn. On the one hand, he felt kind of safe

and protected inside the reinforced barrel. On the other hand, he didn't want to go through that ride again.

Overton Hill dropped through the roof of the Cooper Works and looked around. "You children don't appear happy yet. Fear not. More fun to come!"

The Hounds of Heck forced them out of the barrels and toward Stonehenge. As they ran along, Elisa puffed out, "We must do something."

"I will get help," C.D. said, and leaped into the air in his bat form. Danny watched over his shoulder as C.D. fluttered toward Great Moments in Brooklyn History. But before he got far, three Hounds of Heck were in the sky swooping after him. The bat tried to avoid them, but the hounds kept diving at him, forcing him to the ground, where he once more took his human form.

"You modern children know a lot of tricks," Overton Hill said. "But you must still have fun. Onward!"

"This is getting a bit thick, isn't it?" Howie shouted to Overton Hill.

"Thick? You call this thick? Why, we've just begun!"

"But it isn't fun," Danny cried.

"It is!" Overton Hill cried back. "It is!"

Howie stopped and turned to face the hounds. He put back his head and gave a mighty howl, a noise Danny thought could send rocks into hiding. The hounds skidded to a stop, and for a moment Danny and his friends rested. But the moment Howie stopped howling, the hounds came on again. Howie howled, and they stopped. "That is fine," C.D. said. Danny and the others started to back away.

"Yes, but I can't keep it up for long." Even while Howie said this, the hounds bounded forward. Howie opened his mouth to howl again, but instead, he yawned. "It's no good," Howie said. The hounds were onto him in a moment. He and the others had to struggle on.

The Hounds of Heck herded them through Stonehenge and across a corner of the Enchanted Forest. The mechanical animals said, "Have fun. Have fun."

"They gave better advice before," Frankie said.

Soon they clattered onto the stone pavement of Adventure Court. The hounds hurried them onto platforms designed to look like flying carpets, and the kids were carried into the Arabian Nights ride.

The carpets might as well have been equipped with rockets, and Danny had to hang on tight to his to keep from being blown off. He and the others flew across an Arabian marketplace and in through the window of the caliph's palace where Aladdin was rubbing his lamp to make a genie appear. Then down into a cavern which opened to them when a mechanical figure of Ali Baba called out in a shrill chipmunk voice, "Open sesame." Inside the cavern were mountains of treasure and at least forty thieves, maybe more. There was no time for Danny to count them.

The ride might have been fun under other circumstances, but they flew from one scene to the next so quickly there was no time to do more than get a glimpse of any of them. Even poor Ali

Baba's voice was running too fast. As the hounds forced him off the flying carpet, Danny's mind was awhirl with impressions.

Howie dropped back to where Danny was trying to keep ahead of the hounds, and he said, "I don't know about you, Danny, but I have been entertained beyond my capacity to enjoy it."

"That's for sure."

Elisa called out, "I have an idea. Follow what I do."

"Why is no one smiling?" Overton Hill called down to them as he floated by.

The hounds loaded the kids aboard stagecoaches and leaped in after them. The hounds put their heads out the windows as the coaches shot into Pecos Bill's Wild West ride, rocking madly. "Smile, can't you?" cried Overton Hill as he floated along behind them.

The coaches charged onto a western street that was complete with mechanical horses and cowboys. A showdown was in progress. The two cowboys fired at each other just as the stagecoach passed between them and banged through the swinging doors of a saloon. According to the sign painted on a cow skull, beyond the saloon was the Painted Desert.

Heat from hidden lamps beat down on them as they raced headlong through a fairly convincing model. Sand in hundreds of shades of red, brown, and yellow spread in waves to the horizon.

"Now," Elisa whispered, and she jumped from the coach. Danny and the others jumped too, rolling across what turned out to be painted cement.

"Hey!" cried Stevie. He and the hounds, still

aboard their careening coach, were looking back at Danny and the monster kids. They slammed through a door in a cactus and released the sound of Indians singing. Danny could see Indians dancing while cavalry soldiers sat around the camp fire and watched. The cactus closed.

Overton Hill dropped to the ground among Danny and the monster kids and said, "You must finish the ride or I'll have the hounds on you." He shook a finger in their faces.

Chapter Nine

A Great Moment in Brooklyn History

Overton Hill and the monster kids confronted one another on the fake desert. Now that he was off the stagecoach, Danny could see things from an angle the designers had never intended. A cactus that from the coach seemed to be bigger than a tree was actually smaller than a fireplug. Mountains were just painted on the back wall. The place just looked like a big cement room that had been painted by someone who needed to have his or her eyes checked. The lamps were still on and Danny was sweating as if he were on a real desert. The heat, at least, was real.

"We are done with rides," Elisa said. "We will cure the curse another way."

"There is no other way," Overton Hill cried.

"Before," said Danny, "you thought there was no way at all."

Overton Hill still pointed his knobby finger at them, but he'd stopped shaking it. He noticed what he was doing, and put his hand down. He said, "I have been haunting this ground for two hundred years. I will wait a few more minutes before I can leave it. But if your other way fails to work, there are many rides left. One of them *must* be fun." He sounded uncertain but hopeful.

"You have missed the point," Frankie said.

"Do not explain it now, Frankie," Elisa said and patted his arm. She had them all sit in a circle on the painted cement while Overton Hill floated nearby with his arms folded across his chest. The cement was warmer than the air. It was funny to think that outside it was snowing.

Howie said, "We haven't anything to focus on."

"Only the name," Elisa said. "Heinrick van Donk. Please hold hands."

Danny reached for Elisa and C.D., each of whom reached for one of the other monster kids. When Frankie and Howie held hands, the circle was tight. "Concentrate," said Elisa. "Concentrate on Heinrick van Donk."

They all mumbled the name. Electricity began to run up Danny's arms and across his shoulders.

"Heinrick van Donk," Elisa said.

One of the heat lamps sputtered and went out. A breeze came from out of nowhere.

In a voice not entirely her own, Elisa said, "Gather round, spirits. Gather round. We are looking for one among you named Heinrick van Donk. Heinrick van Donk."

The breeze blew harder and became a wind. It blew their hair around. Then Danny heard a voice coming from the end of a long tunnel. "Curse you, Overton Hill. Curse you."

Somebody whimpered. Danny opened his eyes

and saw Overton Hill cringing behind a buffalo no larger than one of his hounds. Over him, a man was spinning in a spiral of smoke that seemed to bore through the sky blue wall over the cement desert.

As the spinning of the man slowed, Danny could see that he was the same man their first seance had attracted. Now, instead of wearing Colonial clothes, he was naked but for a towel he was clutching around his middle. Soon, he floated over the center of their circle, dripping wet. Drops of ghost water fell from his feet and left dry ghost puddles.

"Timing is everything," Howie said.

"I was clean making," the man in the towel said angrily. "Who for Heinrick van Donk calls?"

"We do," said Elisa in her strange deep voice. Her eyes were still closed.

"Children," said Heinrick van Donk, disgusted.

"And Overton Hill," said Elisa.

"Ja?" said Heinrick van Donk, suddenly interested.

"Show yourself, Overton Hill," Elisa said.

Nothing happened. Then slowly, like a kind of scruffy moon, Overton Hill rose over the mechanical buffalo. He hung there looking shriveled. It was difficult to believe that just moments before he had been flinging his hands around, making demands.

The two ghosts looked at each other. And though Heinrick van Donk was dressed only in a towel, he was the one with more dignity. He sneered and said, "A long time it has been, Overton."

"Two centuries, as I figure it."

Van Donk almost laughed. Instead, he said, "It's true. One for figuring you always were."

Elisa said, "Overton Hill has done his time. Release him from his accursed state."

A single syllable of laughter exploded from van Donk.

"We must have more rides," Overton Hill said, rumbling like faraway thunder.

"What have you got against Overton Hill?" Howie said. His voice, though normal, quivered a little.

"What against him have I?" van Donk roared. "The most nasty old skinflint he is. Having a good time he is not, and allowing others a good time he is not." He looked through the ceiling into the past. "My theater he closed. And all for to put up a stinking pit of a glue factory." He pointed outside. "Yonder it was. Where the massive sham tree now stands."

"Business is business," Overton Hill said.

Van Donk said, "I see that nothing you have learned in your two centuries. Stay cursed." He turned and the smoke spiral began to twist around him.

"Wait," Elisa cried. And this time Heinrick van Donk waited. She said, "This cannot go on."

"It can. *Ja.*"

Elisa opened her eyes and a tear rolled from one of them. She gazed at Overton Hill and said, "Say you are sorry."

Overton Hill raised his fists and shook one of them at Heinrick van Donk. "Sorry for what? For doing my business as I see fit?" More quietly, he said to Elisa, "Better he should apologize to me for my trouble. It is not easy haunting. It is no picnic to be cursed."

"A picnic it was not meant to be. I go."

"Wait," Danny cried.

"*Ja?*" said van Donk, tired of the whole thing.

"You both want the Wonder Hill Amusement Park to be a success, don't you?"

"It matters not."

"I'd make it a glue factory again if I could."

"No, listen," said Danny. "Mr. van Donk, you should want the park to open because people will have fun here. Don't you want people to have fun?"

"*Ja.*" Van Donk sounded as if he were ready to be persuaded.

Danny went on: "And you, Mr. Hill. Remember, if the park doesn't open because you're haunting it, nobody will ever have a good time here and you'll be cursed forever. They'll probably knock this place down and turn it into . . ." Danny tried to think of the place Overton Hill would enjoy least.

"A parking lot?" Howie said.

"Yeah," said Danny. "A parking lot. How'd you like to haunt a parking lot, Mr. Hill?"

For a moment nobody said anything. Overton Hill and Heinrick van Donk were pulling at their lower lips as they thought. With a look of unconcern, Overton Hill said, "You were a menace to art."

"Menace how?"

"If only you hadn't put on that terrible production of *Macbeth*."

"Terrible it was not. A new interpretation it was."

"Terrible," said Overton Hill.

"It was not. Shakespeare you may ask—yourself."

At first the importance of Heinrick van Donk's offer was lost on Overton Hill. Then he said, "You mean—?"

"*Ja, ja*. To the *kinder* the park we leave. Open, it will. A good time by all will be had."

Overton Hill puffed himself up and gave a shrill whistle with his two fingers. A moment later the Hounds of Heck leaped through the walls into the Painted Desert room. They milled around, barking and grumbling. The spiral of smoke gathered around Heinrick van Donk, and Overton Hill joined him at its center. The spiral began to glow pink.

"I still say you cannot do *Macbeth* dressed as George Washington."

"George himself you will ask. And burgher Shakespeare too."

The two men whirled away, and the Hounds of Heck bayed as they were sucked in after, like autumn leaves sucked into a vacuum cleaner. The sound faded to the hiss of air-conditioning. The smoke wound down its ghostly drain.

The electricity was gone from Danny's limp body. The kids were alone. They held hands just for the comfort of it. Danny's were not the only ones that were shaking.

Frankie said, "Stevie Brickwald is much like Overton Hill."

"Yes," said C.D. "Stevie must be a throwout."

"That's throwback," Danny said. He playfully punched C.D. in the shoulder.

"But I do not understand," C.D. said. "When they left, Overton Hill and Heinrick van Donk were still arguing."

"At least they were talking," Howie said. "That's progress."

"The important part," Frankie said, "is that the park is no longer haunted. It will open on schedule and people will have fun."

They waited for Elisa to awaken, and when she did, she wanted water. They might have been in the real desert for all the water there was.

Quickly, they followed the stagecoach tracks out of the ride. Nothing looked convincing. The mechanical people and animals were stiff. Still it was weird that the robots all looked as if they were just about to move.

Stevie was waiting for Danny and the others in front. He was wearing an Indian war bonnet, and he seemed a little confused. "Hi, guys," he said.

"How you doing, Stevie?" Danny said. "Great hat."

"Hm?" He felt the feathers and grinned. "Yeah," he said. "It was part of the peace ceremony. Great ride, huh?" He looked behind them. "Where's Overton Hill and his hounds?"

"Gone," said Howie.

"Gone?"

C.D. said, "Back to wherever ghosts go when they go."

"That's great," said Stevie.

They walked back across the park and stopped at a drinking fountain shaped like a flower. Elisa took big gulps from it and some of the water rolled down her chin.

"You OK, Elisa?" Stevie Brickwald said.

"Much better now, thank you."

They walked on, and a mechanical bird in the enchanted forest said, "Work hard and keep your promises."

In the middle of Stonehenge, Stevie said, "Listen, guys, uh, thanks for saving me."

C.D. bowed to Stevie and Stevie bowed back. Danny said, "This must be one of those great moments in Brooklyn history."

"I guess it is. Just one thing," Stevie said. "I'd appreciate it if you don't tell anybody I thanked you. I mean, I have my reputation to think about."

Howie said, "Why you ungrateful—"

Elisa interrupted him. "It would be our pleasure," she said.

Howie glared at her for a moment, looked at Stevie, and shrugged. He said, "Perhaps we all have reputations to think about."

"What do you mean by that, fur-face?" Stevie showed his fist to Howie.

Howie said, "As I thought." Stevie laughed nervously, and put his fist away.

When they got to Great Moments in Brooklyn History, Stevie went in first. "Just for the look of things," he said.

When they could wait no longer, Danny and his friends followed. Stevie was explaining where he'd been to Ms. Cosgrove and Mr. Hill and the students. "Those hounds aren't so tough," he said.

When he saw Danny and the others, he said, "Where you guys been hiding?" He laughed in his old nasty way.

"Ms. Cosgrove," Arthur Finster called from the WONDER WORKERS ONLY door. "The telephone has a dial tone again."

"You see?" said Mr. Hill. "Everything is fine. I'll bet you can open the doors too."

"Will you check for us, Howie?"

"Delighted," Howie said as he ran from the theater.

While he was gone, Stevie explained how he had gotten away from Overton Hill and the hounds. "I out thought 'em. I out maneuvered 'em."

"But where are they?" Ms. Cosgrove said.

"Probably under the same rock they crawled out from."

Stevie punched Jason Nickles, and Jason said, "Yeah, the same rock."

Ms. Cosgrove was a little confused. She said, "You mean you had to escape from special effects?"

Stevie glanced at Elisa. She shrugged. Stevie said, "They were really good effects."

Howie ran into the theater and said, "I was able to push one of the doors open. It has stopped snowing."

Mr. Hill was as pleased as if he'd stopped the snow himself. He said, "There you go, Ms. Cosgrove. I guess that takes care of everything."

"I guess it does, Mr. Hill. The question is, have we had enough excitement for one day or do we still want to see the rest of Wonder Hill?"

"Wonder Hill," her class shouted—all the class

87

except a few who had seen quite a bit of the park already.

"Very well," Ms. Cosgrove said. "Mr. Hill?"

"Have fun," he said and made shooing motions.

The class cheered. Jason Nickles ran up the aisle. "Oh boy, rides!" he said. "Come on, Stevie."

He waited, but Stevie shook his head and said, "Naw. You go ahead. These rides are for wimps."

MEL GILDEN is the author of the acclaimed *The Return of Captain Conquer,* published by Houghton Mifflin in 1986. His second novel, *Harry Newberry Says His Mom Is a Superhero,* will be published soon by Henry Holt and Company. Prior to these novels, Gilden had short stories published in such places as *Twilight Zone—The Magazine, The Magazine of Fantasy and Science Fiction,* and many original and reprint anthologies. He is also the author of five previous hair-raising Avon Camelot adventures featuring Danny Keegan and his fifth grade monster friends, *M Is For Monster, Born To Howl, The Pet Of Frankenstein, Z Is For Zombie,* and *Monster Mashers*.

JOHN PIERARD is a freelance illustrator living in Manhattan. He is best known for his science fiction illustrations for *Isaac Asimov's Science Fiction Magazine, Distant Stars,* and SPI games such as Universe. He is co-illustrator of Time Machine #4: *Sail With Pirates* and Time Traveler #3: *The First Settlers,* and is illustrator of Time Machine #11: *Mission to World War II,* Time Machine #15: *Flame of the Inquisition,* and the "Fifth Grade Monsters" series: *M Is For Monster, Born to Howl, The Pet Of Frankenstein, There's A Batwing In My Lunchbox, Z Is For Zombie,* and *Monster Mashers*.

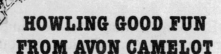

HOWLING GOOD FUN
FROM AVON CAMELOT

Meet the 5th graders of P.S. 13—
the craziest, creepiest kids ever!

THINGS THAT GO BARK IN THE PARK
                              75786-9/$2.75 US/$3.25 CAN

YUCKERS!   75787-7/$2.75 US/$3.25 CAN

M IS FOR MONSTER
                              75423-1/$2.75 US/$3.25 CAN

BORN TO HOWL   75425-8/$2.50 US/$3.25 CAN

THERE'S A BATWING IN MY LUNCHBOX
                              75426-6/$2.75 US/$3.25 CAN

THE PET OF FRANKENSTEIN
                  75185-2/$2.50 US/$2.50 US/$3.25 CAN

Z IS FOR ZOMBIE 75686-2/$2.75 US/$3.25 CAN

MONSTER MASHERS
                  75785-0/$2.75 US/$3.25 CAN